Agatha Christie

*The Witness for the Prosecution*

*and other stories*

**Collins**

# Collins

HarperCollins Publishers
The News Building
1 London Bridge Street
London SE1 9GF

www.collinselt.com

This *Collins English Readers* edition first published by HarperCollins Publishers 2017.

10 9 8 7 6 5 4 3 2 1

www.agathachristie.com

ISBN: 978-0-00-824971-7

A catalogue record for this book is available from the British Library.

Cover design © HarperCollins*Publishers* Ltd/Agatha Christie Ltd 2017

Typeset by Davidson Publishing Solutions, Glasgow

Printed and bound by CPI Group (UK) Ltd., Croydon, CR0 4YY

# *Contents*

# ♦ INTRODUCTION ♦

## ABOUT COLLINS ENGLISH READERS

*Collins English Readers* have been created for readers worldwide whose first language is not English. The stories are carefully graded to ensure that you, the reader, will both enjoy and benefit from your reading experience.

Words which are above the required reading level are underlined the first time they appear in a story. All underlined words are defined in the **Glossary** at the back of the book. Books at levels 1 and 2 take their definitions from the *Collins COBUILD Essential English Dictionary*, and books at levels 3 and above from the *Collins COBUILD Advanced English Dictionary*. Where appropriate, definitions are simplified for level and context.

Alongside the glossary, a **Character list** is provided to help the reader identify who is who, and how they are connected to each other. **Cultural notes** explain historical, cultural and other references. **Maps and diagrams** are provided where appropriate. A **downloadable recording** is also available of the full story. To access the audio, go to www.collinselt.com/eltreadersaudio. The password is the last word on page 3 of this book.

To support both teachers and learners, additional materials are available online at www.collinselt.com/readers. These include a **Plot synopsis** and **classroom activities** (both for teachers), **Student activities**, a **level checker** and much more.

## About Agatha Christie

Agatha Christie (1890–1976) is known throughout the world as the Queen of Crime. She is the most widely published and translated author of all time and in any language; only the Bible and Shakespeare have sold more copies.

Agatha Christie's first novel was published in 1920. It featured Hercule Poirot, the Belgian detective who has become the most popular detective in crime fiction since Sherlock Holmes.

Collins has published Agatha Christie since 1926.

## The Grading Scheme

The Collins COBUILD Grading Scheme has been created using the most up-to-date language usage information available today. Each level is guided by a comprehensive grammar and vocabulary framework, ensuring that the series will perfectly match readers' abilities.

| | | CEF band | Pages | Word count | Headwords |
|---|---|---|---|---|---|
| Level 1 | elementary | A2 | 64 | 5,000–8,000 | approx. 700 |
| Level 2 | pre-intermediate | A2–B1 | 80 | 8,000–11,000 | approx. 900 |
| Level 3 | intermediate | B1 | 96 | 11,000–20,000 | approx. 1,300 |
| Level 4 | upper-intermediate | B2 | 112-128 | 15,000–26,000 | approx. 1,700 |
| Level 5 | upper-intermediate+ | B2+ | 128+ | 22,000–30,000 | approx. 2,200 |
| Level 6 | advanced | C1 | 144+ | 28,000+ | 2,500+ |
| Level 7 | advanced+ | C2 | 160+ | *varied* | *varied* |

For more information on the Collins COBUILD Grading Scheme go to www.collinselt.com/readers/gradingscheme.

# The Witness for the Prosecution

◆ ◆ ◆

Mr Mayherne was a small man. He had clever grey eyes, wore good quality clothes and he always looked neat and tidy. Everybody knew that he was a very good lawyer[1].

Mayherne touched his glasses and coughed. He always did this when he was thinking. Then he looked again at the man sitting opposite him, the man charged with murder.

He felt a little sorry for his client.

'This is very serious. You must be completely honest with me.'

Leonard Vole looked at him miserably.

'I know,' he said in a hopeless voice. 'You keep telling me that it's serious. But I just can't believe that I'm charged with murder – *murder*.'

'Yes, yes, yes,' he said.

Mayherne was not emotional – he was a sensible man. He coughed again, took off his glasses, cleaned them carefully, and put them back on his nose.

'Now, my dear Mr Vole, I'm going to try very hard to prove that you're innocent – and I will succeed – *we* will succeed. But I must have all the facts.'

The young man still looked at him in the same confused, hopeless way.

'You think I'm guilty,' said Leonard Vole. 'But I promise, I'm not! I didn't do it, Mr Mayherne. I didn't!'

Even though Mr Mayherne knew that any man in his position would say the same, he thought maybe Leonard Vole might really be innocent.

'You're right, Mr Vole,' he said in a serious voice. 'The <u>case</u> against you looks very bad. But I believe you. Now, let's talk about the facts. I want you to tell me exactly how you met Miss Emily French.'

'It was in Central London. I saw an elderly lady crossing the road. She was carrying a lot of parcels and she dropped them in the middle of the street. She tried to pick them up but a bus came along and she had to rush to the pavement. Then I picked up the parcels for her.'

'Did you save her life?'

'Oh no! All I did was pick up the parcels, but she was very grateful. She thanked me and said something about me being more helpful than most young people – I can't remember the exact words. I said goodbye and went on with my day. I never expected to see her again.

'But life is full of surprises. That same evening, I met her again at a party. She recognized me. I then found out that she was Miss Emily French and that she lived at Cricklewood. I talked to her for a while. I think Emily French was a lady who decided quickly whether she liked someone. She decided that she liked me because I had helped her, but anyone would have done the same. She asked me to come and visit her some time – I said, of course, that I would. I didn't particularly want to go, but it would have been rude to refuse. She asked me when, so I said I would go the following Saturday.

'After she'd gone, my friends told me that she was rich and that she lived alone with just a <u>maid</u>.'

'I see,' said Mayherne. 'So you knew she was rich soon after you'd met her?'

Leonard Vole was angry. 'If you mean did I ask if she was rich—' he began, but Mayherne interrupted him.

'I have to look at the case the way the <u>prosecution</u> will explain it in <u>court</u>[1]. Miss French didn't look rich, she didn't spend much money or have many things. Unless someone told you, you would probably have thought that she was poor. Who was it who told you that she had money?'

'My friend, George Harvey. It was his party.'

'Will he remember telling you?'

'I really don't know. It was a while ago.'

'Mr Vole, the prosecution will show that you needed money – that is true, isn't it?'

Leonard Vole looked embarrassed.

'Yes,' he said quietly.

'So, they'll say you needed money and you met this rich old lady and tried hard to develop a friendship with her. Now, if we can say that you didn't know that she was rich, and that you visited her to be kind—'

'Which is true.'

'I'm sure it is. But remember I'm looking at it like the prosecution will do. So, it's important to know what Mr Harvey remembers. Is he likely to remember that conversation, or not? Could we make him think that the conversation took place later?'

Leonard Vole thought for a moment. Then he said:

'No, I don't think that that would be successful, Mr Mayherne. Several people heard him tell me at the party.'

The lawyer tried to hide his disappointment.

'That's unfortunate,' he said. 'But thank you for being honest, Mr Vole. You're quite right – that won't work.

'So, you met Miss French, you visited her at her home, and a friendship developed. We need to give a good reason for all this. Why did you, a young man of thirty-three, good-looking, good at sports, popular with your friends, spend so much time with an elderly woman? You must have had hardly anything in common.'

Leonard Vole looked nervous. 'I don't know – I really don't know. After the first visit, she asked me to come again. It was clear that she liked me. She said she was lonely and unhappy, so it was difficult to say no.

'You see, Mr Mayherne, I'm one of those people who can't say no. And believe it or not, after the third or fourth visit I really did start to like her. My mother died when I was young, and I was brought up by an aunt who died before I was fifteen. If I told you that I enjoyed her acting like a mother to me, I think you'd laugh.'

Mayherne didn't laugh. Instead he took off his glasses again and cleaned them. This was always a sign that he was thinking.

'I believe you, Mr Vole,' he said at last. 'I just don't know whether a jury[1] would.

'Please continue. When did Miss French first ask for your advice about business?'

'After my third or fourth visit. She didn't understand very much about money, and was worried about some investments.'

Mayherne looked up quickly.

'Be careful, Mr Vole. The maid, Janet Mackenzie, says that Miss French was a good businesswoman, and her bank manager agrees.'

'I can't help that,' said Vole seriously. 'That's what she said to me.'

This answer made Mayherne believe Leonard Vole even more. He knew a little about elderly ladies. He could imagine Miss French, enjoying the company of the good-looking young man, trying to find reasons for him to visit her. Of course she would say that she didn't understand business and ask him to help her. She knew that most men like to be asked for help. Leonard Vole had liked being asked. Perhaps she had wanted this young man to know that she was rich. Perhaps Emily French had been willing to pay for what she wanted.

All these thoughts passed quickly through Mayherne's mind, but he didn't show it. Instead, he asked another question.

'And did you help her when she asked you to?'

'I did.'

'Mr Vole,' said the lawyer, 'I'm going to ask you a very serious question, and it's important that you tell me the truth. You needed money. You were helping an old lady with her investments – an old lady who said she knew little or nothing about business. Did you at any time, or in any way, move any of Emily French's investments or money to your own accounts—?

'Now, wait a minute before you answer. We have two options. Either we concentrate on you being honest. We explain that it's unlikely that you would murder Miss French as you could have easily taken her money anyway. However, if the prosecution can prove that you swindled the old lady in any way, we must instead say that you had no reason to murder her, since you already had her money. Do you understand the difference?

'Now, please think carefully before you answer.'

But Leonard Vole answered quickly.

'I did not swindle Miss French.'

'Thank you,' said Mayherne. 'I'm pleased to hear that. I know that you're far too clever to lie to me about such an important thing.'

'Good! So,' said Vole with excitement, 'the strongest point in my case is that I have no reason to have hurt her. Yes, I developed a friendship with a rich old lady. Yes, I suppose I hoped to get some money from a friendship with her, but isn't it clear that her death has ended all my hopes?'

The lawyer looked at him seriously. Then, he repeated his habit of cleaning his glasses. He didn't speak until they were back on his nose.

'Do you not know, Mr Vole, that Miss French left a <u>will</u> and that in her will she leaves most of her money to you?'

'What?' The prisoner jumped to his feet. 'What are you saying? She left her money to me?'

Mayherne <u>nodded</u> his head slowly.

Vole sat down again. He put his head in his hands.

'You didn't know anything about this will?'

'No, I knew nothing about it.'

'What would you say if I told you that the maid, Janet Mackenzie, says that you did know? She says that Miss French told her that she had talked to you about it.'

'What would I say?' Leonard Vole repeated. 'I'd say that she's lying! No, no that isn't fair. Janet loved Miss French, and she didn't like me. She was jealous and <u>suspicious</u> of me. Perhaps Miss French told Janet what she was going to do, and Janet either didn't understand properly, or convinced herself that I had persuaded the old lady to do it.'

'Do you think she dislikes you enough to lie in court?'

Leonard Vole looked shocked. 'No! Why would she?'

'I don't know,' said Mayherne. 'But she really doesn't like you.'

'I'm beginning to see,' Leonard Vole said quietly. 'The prosecution will say that I encouraged the friendship, that I got her to make a will leaving her money to me, and then that I went to her house that night, and there was nobody else there – then they find her dead the next day – oh! It's awful!'

'You're wrong about there being nobody else in the house,' said Mayherne, moving the conversation on. 'Janet was planning to go out for the evening. She did go out, but at about half past nine she returned home to get something she had forgotten. She came in through the back door, went upstairs and fetched it, and went out again. She heard voices in the sitting room. She couldn't hear what they were saying, but she's sure that one of them was Miss French's voice and the other was a man's.'

'At half past nine,' said Leonard Vole, thinking. 'At half past nine...'

He jumped to his feet again. 'Then I'm saved – saved!'

'What do you mean, saved?' asked Mayherne, surprised.

'*By half past nine I was at home again!* My wife can prove that. I left Miss French at about five minutes to nine. I arrived home at about twenty past nine. My wife was there waiting for me. Oh, thank goodness – thank goodness! And thanks to Janet Mackenzie for forgetting something.'

Leonard Vole was so happy, he didn't notice that Mayherne still looked serious.

'Who do you think murdered Miss French, then?' asked the lawyer.

'A burglar, of course. The window was open, wasn't it? She was killed with a crowbar, and the crowbar was found lying on the floor beside the body. And several things were missing. After all, the police first thought it was a burglar. It's only because Janet told the police she was suspicious of me that I was charged.'

'That's not good enough, Mr Vole,' said the lawyer. 'The things that were missing were cheap. Someone took them to make it look like it was a burglar.

'Besides, think about it. You say you weren't in the house at half past nine. So who was the man Janet heard talking to

Miss French in the sitting room? She wouldn't have a friendly conversation with a burglar, would she?'

'No,' said Vole. 'No...' He looked confused.

'But anyway,' he added suddenly looking happier again, 'it means it wasn't me. I've got an <u>alibi</u>. You must see Romaine – my wife – as soon as possible.'

'Certainly,' said the lawyer. 'I would have already seen Mrs Vole, but she's been away since you were charged. I believe that she arrives back tonight, so I'm going to see her when I leave here.'

Vole nodded, satisfied.

'Yes, Romaine will tell you. How lucky is that?'

'Excuse me, Mr Vole, but are you very fond of your wife?'

'Of course!'

'And is she fond of you?'

'Romaine loves me very much. She'd do anything for me.'

The lawyer's hopes grew smaller. A wife in love with her husband – would a jury really believe her?

'Was there anyone else who saw you return at 9.20? A maid, for instance?'

'No, we don't have a maid.'

'Did you meet anyone in the street on the way back?' 'Nobody I knew. I took the bus part of the way. The driver might remember me.'

Mayherne doubted this.

'There isn't anyone else, then, who can say when you arrived home?'

'No. But is that necessary?'

'Maybe not. Maybe not,' said Mayherne quickly.

He continued: 'Now, there's just one more thing. Did Miss French know that you were a married man?'

'Oh, yes.'

'Yet you never took your wife to see her. Why was that?'

For the first time, Leonard Vole was slow to answer.

'Well – I don't know.'

'Janet Mackenzie says that Miss French believed that you were single, and that she talked about marrying you.'

Vole laughed.

'There was forty years' difference in age between us.'

'It has been done before,' said the lawyer, not laughing. 'The fact is that your wife never met Miss French?'

'No…' Again the answer was slow.

'I must say,' said the lawyer, 'I don't understand why they never met.'

Vole looked embarrassed.

'I'll be honest. I needed money, as you know. I hoped that Miss French might lend me some. She was fond of me, but she wasn't at all interested in a young couple's problems. I soon realized that she thought that my wife and I didn't get on – that we weren't living together. Mr Mayherne, I wanted the money – for Romaine. So, I didn't say anything. I let the old lady think what she wanted. She said I was like a son to her. There was never any conversation about marriage – that must be just Janet's imagination.'

'And that's all?'

'Yes – that's all.'

Did Leonard Vole pause before he said that, Mayherne wondered? He couldn't tell. He stood up and held out his hand.

'Goodbye, Mr Vole.'

He looked into Leonard's tired young face and, without planning to, said, 'In spite of the many facts against you, I believe you're innocent. I hope to prove it.'

Vole smiled at him.

'You'll see that my alibi is true,' he said. He hardly noticed that the lawyer didn't smile back.

Mayherne said, 'I think what Janet Mackenzie tells the jury is very important. She hates you. That much is clear.'

'Oh, no! She dislikes me, but I don't think she *hates* me,' said the young man. The lawyer shook his head as he went out. He was unhappy with the way the case was developing.

'Now to visit Mrs Vole,' he said to himself.

◆ ◆ ◆

The Voles lived in a small, shabby house near Paddington Green. Mayherne rang the bell when he arrived.

A big woman in dirty clothes answered the door.

'I'm looking for Mrs Vole. Is she home yet?'

'She got back an hour ago. But I don't know if you can see her.'

'Please tell her it's Mr Mayherne,' said the lawyer quietly. 'I'm sure she will see me.'

The woman closed the door in his face and left him waiting outside.

In a few minutes, however, she returned and was a little nicer to him.

'Come inside, please.'

She took him into a tiny sitting room. Mayherne, who was looking at a drawing on the wall, jumped as he noticed a tall, pale woman who had entered so quietly that he hadn't heard her.

'Mr Mayherne? You're my husband's lawyer, aren't you? Will you please sit down?' When she spoke, he realized that she was not English. Now, looking at her more closely, he noticed that she was a pretty woman, and that she made little movements with her hands that made her seem nervous. A strange woman, very quiet. She made him want to leave.

'My dear Mrs Vole,' he began, 'you mustn't worry—'

He stopped. He realized, with surprise, that it was very obvious that Romaine Vole was not at all worried. She was perfectly calm.

'Please tell me all about it,' she said. 'I must know everything. How bad is it?' She stopped for a second, then repeated in a quieter, stranger voice: 'How bad is it?'

Mayherne described his interview with Leonard Vole. She listened, nodding her head as she did.

'I see,' she said, when he had finished. 'So he wants me to say that he came in at twenty minutes past nine that night?'

'*Did* he come in at that time?' asked Mayherne quickly.

'That isn't the point,' she said. 'If I say he did, will they find him innocent? Will they believe me?'

Mayherne was shocked. She had jumped to the heart of the situation so quickly.

'That's what I want to know,' she said. 'Will it be enough? Is there anyone else who can also speak for him in court?'

The way she said this made him feel worried.

He didn't want to admit it, but he had no choice: 'So far there is no one else.'

'I see,' said Romaine Vole.

She sat perfectly still for a minute or two. There was a little smile on her lips.

The lawyer grew more and more worried. 'Mrs Vole,' he began. 'I know what you must feel—'

'Do you?' she asked. 'I wonder.'

'In the situation you find yourself in—'

'In the situation I find myself in,' she interrupted him, 'I'm going to make my own decision about what I do.'

He was very worried now.

'But, my dear Mrs Vole – you're obviously upset. As you love your husband—'

'Pardon?'

Her voice made him jump. He repeated more slowly:

'As you love your husband...'

Romaine nodded slowly, a strange smile on her lips.

'Did he tell you that I love him?' she asked in a soft voice. 'Yes, I can see that he did. How stupid men are! Stupid, stupid, stupid.'

She stood up suddenly.

'I hate him, I tell you! I hate him, I hate him, I hate him! I'd like to see him <u>hanged</u>[2].'

The lawyer stepped backwards, shocked.

She moved a step nearer to him: 'Perhaps I *will* see it. What if I tell you that he didn't come in that night at twenty past nine, but at twenty past *ten*? He tells you he knew nothing about the money in the will. What if I tell you he knew all about it, and he murdered her to get it? What if I tell you that he told me what he'd done that night when he got home? That there was blood on his clothes? What then? What if I say all these things in court?'

With an effort, Mayherne hid his feelings and tried to speak calmly.

'A wife can't give <u>evidence</u> against her husband—'

'He isn't my husband!'

She said the words so quickly that he wondered if he had heard them correctly.

'Pardon? I—'

'He isn't my husband.'

In the silence that followed, <u>you could have heard a pin drop</u>.

'I was an actress in Vienna before I met Leonard. I'm married, but my husband is in a <u>psychiatric</u> hospital. So Leonard and I couldn't get married. My real name is Romaine Heilger.'

Mayherne tried to quickly understand everything she was saying, thinking only of the case.

'I'd like you to tell me one thing,' he said. 'Why do you hate Leonard Vole so much?'

She smiled.

'Yes, I'm sure you'd like to know. But I won't tell you. It's my secret…'

Equally confused and annoyed, Mayherne stood up. 'Then there is no point in continuing this conversation,' he said. 'You'll hear from me again after I've spoken with my client.'

She came closer to him, looking into his eyes with her own beautiful dark ones.

'Tell me,' she said. 'Did you honestly believe that he was innocent when you came here today?'

'I did,' said Mayherne.

'You poor little man,' she laughed.

'And I still believe he is,' finished the lawyer. She looked surprised.

'Good evening, madam.' He left.

'This is going to be very difficult,' said Mr Mayherne to himself as he walked quickly along the street away from the house.

The whole case was extraordinary. And she was an extraordinary woman – and a very dangerous one.

What could he do? That poor young man had no chance now. Of course, it was possible that he was guilty…

'No,' said Mayherne to himself. 'No – there's almost too much evidence against him. I don't believe this woman. She was making up the whole story. But she'll never tell it in court.'

He just wished he felt more sure about this.

◆ ◆ ◆

Mayherne didn't know what to do. The case against Leonard Vole was looking very bad. Even the famous court lawyer Sir Charles, who Mayherne had employed to speak for Vole in court[1], was not very hopeful.

'Our only chance,' he told them, 'is to show that Romaine is lying. But how?'

Mayherne tried to think. If Leonard Vole was telling the truth, and he did leave the murdered woman's house at nine o'clock, then who was the man Janet had heard talking to Miss French at half past nine?

Then no one had seen Leonard Vole leaving Miss French's house or entering his own house. No one had seen any other man enter or leave Miss French's house either. So how could he prove what Vole had told him about his movements?

Mayherne had no more ideas.

Days passed, and Mayherne still had no plan for how to prove his client was innocent.

Then, the day before the <u>trial</u>, he received a letter that changed everything. It was written very badly on cheap, old paper. The envelope was dirty and the stamp was stuck in the wrong place.

*Dear Mister:*
*You're the lawyer who is working for the young man. If you want to show what that awful woman is really like and that everything she says is a lie, come to 16 Shaw's Rents, Stepney, tonight. It'll cost you 200 pounds. Ask for Mrs Mogson.*

The lawyer read and re-read this strange letter. Was it real? He thought it probably was. He also thought it was Vole's only hope.

Mayherne made up his mind. It was his job to try to save his client. He had to go and meet this lady.

When he arrived at Shaw's Rents that night, it was a horrible place. He asked for number 16 and was sent up to a room on the third floor. He knocked on the door. There was no answer, so he knocked again.

At this second knock, he heard a sound inside. He waited and the door opened a few centimetres.

Suddenly he heard a woman's laugh from inside, and the door opened wider. He still couldn't see anyone.

'So it's you,' she said, in a low voice from behind the door. 'There's nobody with you, is there? Then you can come in.'

Although he didn't really want to, the lawyer stepped into the small, dirty, dark room. There was an untidy bed in a corner, a plain table and two old chairs. Mayherne looked at the woman as she followed him into the room. She was middle-aged, with lots of unbrushed grey hair and a scarf covering most of her face. She saw him looking at this and she laughed again.

'I suppose you're wondering why I hide my beauty? Hah, I'll show you.'

She removed the scarf and the lawyer stepped backwards, shocked. Her face was covered with a huge red <u>scar</u>.

She laughed again, then put the scarf back on.

'And yet I was a pretty girl once – not as long ago as you'd think. <u>Acid</u> – that's what did it. But they'll be sorry...'

He noticed her hands opening and closing angrily.

'Enough,' said the lawyer. 'I've come here because I believe you can give me information which will help my client, Leonard Vole. Is that correct?'

'What about the money?' she said. 'Two hundred pounds, you remember?'

'Now, listen. It's your duty to tell me, and I can make you tell me in court if I have to.'

'Oh no, that won't happen. You see, I'm getting old, and I don't remember anything. But if you give me two hundred pounds, perhaps I can remember something...'

'What?'

'A letter from *her*. But before I'll say more, I want my money.'

Mayherne made up his mind.

'I'll give you ten pounds, and nothing more. And only if this letter you talk about is helpful and real.'

'Ten pounds?' She screamed at him.

'Twenty,' said Mayherne, 'and that's my last offer.'

He stood up, ready to leave if she refused. Then, watching her closely, he took out his wallet, and counted out twenty pounds.

'You see?' he said. 'This is all I have with me. You can take it or leave it.'

But already he knew that the sight of the money was too much for her. She complained, but she went over to the bed and took something out from under it.

'Here you are!' she said angrily, throwing him a pile of letters. 'You need the top one.'

Mayherne read each letter through calmly, then returned again to the top one and read it a second time.

They were love letters, written by Romaine Heilger – but the man they were written to was not Leonard Vole...

'I was telling the truth, wasn't I?' said the woman. 'Those letters prove she's lying, don't they?'

Mayherne put the letters in his pocket.

The woman hadn't finished. 'I know something else too,' she said. 'You must find out where *Romaine* was at twenty past ten – the time she says she was at home. Ask at the Lion Road Cinema.'

'Who's the man she wrote all these letters to?' asked Mayherne. 'There's only a first name here.'

The woman's voice changed, her hands opened and closed again. Finally she lifted one hand to her face. 'He's the man that did this to me. *She* took him away from me. And when I tried to get him back, he threw acid at me. And she laughed! I've hated them for years. I've followed them and watched them. And now they'll be sorry. What will happen to her, Mr Lawyer? Something bad?'

'Yes, she'll probably go to prison for lying in court,' said Mayherne, standing up calmly and quietly.

'Good – that's what I want. Are you leaving? Where's my money?'

Without a word, Mayherne put the money down on the table. Then, taking a deep breath, he turned and left the awful room.

He went straight to the Lion Road Cinema. He showed a photograph of Romaine Heilger to the man in the ticket office who recognized her immediately. She had arrived at the cinema with a man a little after ten o'clock. He couldn't remember the man very well, but he remembered the woman. She had spoken to him about the film. They stayed until the end, about an hour later.

So, everything Romaine Heilger had said was a lie, from beginning to end. She had only said it because she hated Leonard Vole. The lawyer wondered whether he would ever know why she hated Vole so much. What had he done to her? He had seemed confused when the lawyer had told him that she had said she hated him. He had said that it wasn't possible – yet Mayherne had thought that perhaps Leonard Vole did know already. He knew, but he wasn't going to tell Mayherne the truth. Mayherne wondered if one day he would learn what their secret was.

The lawyer glanced at his watch. It was late – he had to hurry.

'I must tell Sir Charles straight away,' he said to himself.

♦ ♦ ♦

The trial of Leonard Vole for the murder of Emily French was very popular. Vole was young and good looking, the crime was nasty, and the public was <u>fascinated</u> by the most important <u>witness</u> for the prosecution, Romaine Heilger. There had been pictures of her in the newspapers, and many different stories <u>made up</u> about her life.

Janet Mackenzie was called first. To begin with, she told the same story as before. Then Sir Charles questioned her and had some success. She admitted that she couldn't be sure that the man's voice she had heard in the sitting room that night was

Vole's. He also managed to show that she was jealous of the prisoner and disliked him.

Then it was the turn of the next witness.

'Is your name Romaine Heilger?'

'Yes.'

'You are Austrian, correct?'

'Yes.'

'But for the last three years you've lived here in England with the prisoner and <u>pretended</u> to be his wife?'

Just for a moment, Romaine Heilger looked at Leonard Vole. Her look was strange. Mayherne couldn't tell what she was thinking.

'Yes.'

The questions continued. She told her story. On that night the prisoner had taken a crowbar with him from their home. He had returned home at twenty minutes past ten, and had told her that he had killed the old lady. His clothes had blood on them, and he had burned them. He had told her to keep his secret or he would hurt her.

As she continued her story, everyone listening began to believe that the prisoner was guilty. Even Leonard Vole looked as if he knew there was no hope for him now.

Then Sir Charles stood up, looking very serious. He began his questions. Mayherne watched from the back of the room. He was nervous. This was the big moment.

Sir Charles suggested that her story was totally made up, from start to finish – that she had not even been in her own house at the time she said Vole came home, that she was in love with another man and that she was trying to send Vole to his death for a crime he did not do.

Then Sir Charles produced the letter. He read it aloud to a silent court.

*Max, my love, I can't believe our luck! Leonard has been arrested for murder – yes, the murder of an old lady! Leonard, who wouldn't hurt a fly! At last I'll have my <u>revenge</u>. I'll say that he came in that night with blood on him – that he told me what he had done. He'll be hanged, Max – and when he hangs he'll know that it was Romaine who sent him to his death. And then – happiness for us, at last!*

When she heard the letter being read, Romaine started to cry and admitted everything. Leonard Vole had returned to the house at the time he said, twenty past nine. She had made up the whole story.

The case for the prosecution was over. The judge reminded the jury to take the time to consider all the evidence, but the jury didn't need much time at all[1].

'We find the prisoner *not guilty*,' they announced.

Mayherne knew that he should immediately go and offer his congratulations to his client.

But instead he found himself cleaning his glasses, and made an effort to stop. His wife had told him the night before that it was becoming a habit. Habits were very strange things, he thought to himself. People never knew they had them.

It had been an interesting case – a very interesting case. That woman, Romaine Heilger...

When he thought about the case, he could think of nothing except her. She had seemed like a pale, quiet woman in the house at Paddington, but in court she had been colourful and lively. She had seemed like a <u>tropical</u> flower in an English garden.

If he closed his eyes he could see her now, tall, calm, her perfect body a little forward, that strange movement with her hands.

Yes, habits were very strange things. Moving her hand like that was her habit, he supposed. Yet he had seen someone else do it quite recently. Who was it? Quite recently...

Suddenly he remembered. *The woman in Shaw's Rents...*

It was impossible – impossible!

Yet, Romaine Heilger was an actress...

Sir Charles came up behind him.

'Have you spoken to our man yet? He's very lucky, you know. Come and see him.'

But the lawyer wanted only one thing – to see Romaine Heilger. And that wouldn't happen for some time.

◆ ◆ ◆

'So you've guessed,' she said, when Mayherne did manage to see her and had told her what he was thinking.

'What do you want to know? The scar on the woman's face? Oh, that was easy – just a bit of make-up, and the light was too bad for you to see it properly.'

'But why— why—?' He didn't know what to say.

'For Leonard – I had to save him. The words of a woman in love with a man would not have been enough for the jury. But if they believed that my evidence was false, that I wanted to hurt the prisoner, then they would feel sorry for him.'

'And why so many letters?'

'If I had only given you one, you probably would have thought it wasn't real.'

'So there never was a man called Max?'

'No, he never existed.'

'Well,' said Mayherne, who was a bit annoyed, 'I still think we could have proved he was innocent by the – er – normal method.'

'Maybe, but I had to be sure. You see, you *thought* he was innocent—'

'And you *knew* it? I see,' said Mayherne.

'Oh no, my dear Mr Mayherne,' said Romaine, smiling. 'You don't see at all. I *knew* he was *guilty*!'

# The Rajah's
# Emerald

◆ ◆ ◆

James Fleming was trying hard to concentrate on the little yellow book in his hand. On its cover it said, 'Do you want your salary increased by 10 per cent per year?' James had just finished reading two pages telling him to look his boss in the face, and to be more <u>dynamic</u> and efficient. It continued: *There is a time to be honest, but there are also times when it is better not to be quite so honest.* The little yellow book also informed him: *A strong man does not always say everything he knows.*

James let the little book close and, raising his head, looked out over the big, blue ocean. He had a horrible feeling that he was not a strong man. A strong man would be in control of his situation, and he didn't feel in control.

This was his holiday, wasn't it? Ha! Who had persuaded him to come to this fashionable seaside resort, Kimpton-on-Sea? Grace. Who had encouraged him to spend more money than he could afford? Grace. And he had happily come.

However, what had happened once she had got him here? While he was staying in a horrible <u>boarding house</u> about a mile and a half from the seafront, Grace had instead found friends staying at the very expensive Esplanade Hotel by the sea and had gone to stay with them! Again James laughed.

He thought back over the last three years of his relationship with Grace. She had been very pleased when he first noticed her. That was before she had been promoted at work. In those early days it had been James who felt important; now, <u>the shoe was on the other foot</u>. Grace was earning good money and it had changed her. Now, she was staying at the Esplanade Hotel, and hardly noticing James was there. She was instead spending her time with Claud Sopworth – a man who James didn't like at all – and his three sisters.

Feeling unhappy, James wondered to himself why he had agreed to come to Kimpton-on-Sea. It was a resort for the rich and fashionable. It had two large hotels, and several miles of pretty houses belonging to fashionable actresses and men who had married rich wives. A week's rent for the smallest house was more than he paid for his London flat for a month. James couldn't imagine how much the rent for the large ones might be.

There was one of these huge houses just behind where James was currently sitting. This one belonged to that famous sportsman Lord[3] Edward Campion, and he had a house full of famous guests including the <u>Rajah</u> of Maraputna, who everyone knew was very, very rich. James had read all about him in the local newspaper that morning: his palaces, his wonderful collection of <u>jewels</u>, including one famous <u>emerald</u> which the papers said was the size of a small egg.

'If I had an emerald like that…' thought James, 'Well, then Grace would be sorry.'

James wasn't really sure what he meant by this, but just saying it made him feel better.

He heard people laughing behind him, and he turned quickly to find Grace there. She was with Clara Sopworth, Alice Sopworth, Dorothy Sopworth and – of course – Claud Sopworth.

'Well, hello stranger,' cried Grace in an annoyed voice.

'Hello,' said James.

He really should have found a better reply. You can't be dynamic with one word.

He looked at Claud Sopworth and hated him. Claud was dressed beautifully. He looked like the hero of a film. James so wanted a big, wet dog to run towards them from the beach and jump up at Claud's perfect white trousers with its wet, sandy feet. James himself was wearing a pair of old, dark-grey trousers that were very far from perfect.

'Isn't the air beautiful here?' said Clara, taking a deep breath. 'It makes you ready for the day, doesn't it?'

She laughed.

'It's the sea,' said Alice. 'Sea air is as good for you as medicine, you know.' And she also laughed.

James thought: 'I'd like to bang their silly heads together. Why are they always laughing? They aren't saying anything funny.'

Perfect Claud said: 'Shall we have a swim, or is everyone too tired?'

The girls loved the idea of swimming. James joined them as they walked down to the beach. He even managed to get Grace on her own, a little behind the others.

'Look, Grace!' he complained, 'I'm hardly seeing you at all.'

'Well, we're all together now,' said Grace, 'and you can come and have lunch with us at the hotel. Although...'

She looked at James's trousers.

'What's the matter?' demanded James, angrily. 'I don't look smart enough for you, I suppose?'

'Well, dear, I do think you could make more of an effort,' said Grace. 'Everyone is so smart here. Look at Claud!'

'I have looked at him,' said James, angrily, 'And I've never seen a man who looked more like a complete ass than he does.'

Grace wasn't happy.

'There's no need to say nasty things about my friends, James – it's not polite. He's dressed just like any other man at the hotel is dressed.'

'Ha!' said James. 'Do you know what I read the other day? That the <u>Duke</u> of... I can't remember where, but a duke, anyway, was the worst dressed man in England!'

'I'm sure,' said Grace, 'but then, you see, he is a duke.'

'So?' demanded James. 'Don't you think I might be a duke one day? Or some other important person?'

He touched the yellow book in his pocket, and started to tell her about lots of men who had done very well even though they had started with less than he had. Grace just laughed.

'Imagine you,' she said. 'Duke of Kimpton-on-Sea! Don't be so silly, James.'

James looked at her, angry and upset. Grace was different here, and he didn't like it.

The sandy beach at Kimpton was very long and straight. There was a huge row of <u>beach huts</u> for about a mile and a half along it. The group had stopped before a row of six huts, all labelled *For visitors to the Esplanade Hotel only.*

'Here we are,' said Grace in a happy voice, 'but I'm afraid you can't come in with us, James – you'll have to go along to the public changing rooms over there. We'll meet you in the sea.'

'OK,' said James, and he walked off.

There were twelve old public changing rooms. James gave the old man who was in charge of them a coin. In return, he gave James a blue ticket, threw a towel to him, and pointed towards a collection of long queues outside each changing room.

'Pick a queue and wait,' he said.

James joined the smallest line of bored, unsmiling people, and waited.

After five minutes, the changing room door opened, and four children and a father and mother came out. The changing room was so small, James wondered how they had all got inside. Immediately two women jumped forward, each trying to get into the changing room first.

'Excuse me,' said the first young woman, breathing quickly.

'Excuse *me*,' said the other young woman, looking angry.

'I was here *ten minutes* before you were,' said the first young woman.

'Anyone will tell you I've been here at least 15 minutes,' said the second young woman.

'Now, now,' said the old man in charge, coming over.

Both young women spoke to him in high, angry voices. When they had finished, he looked at the second young woman, and said:

'It's yours.'

Then he walked away without another word. He didn't know or care who had been there first, but his decision was final.

James grabbed his arm.

'Hey!'

'Yes, mister?'

'How long is it going to be before I get a changing room?'

'Might be an hour, might be an hour and a half, I can't say.'

At that moment James saw Grace and the Sopworth girls running happily down the sand towards the sea.

'Already!' said James to himself. 'Oh, dear!'

He spoke to the old man again.

'Can I get a changing room anywhere else? What about one of these huts along here? They all seem empty.'

'Those huts are private,' said the old man.

Angry now, James left the waiting groups, and walked down the beach. Why should the rich have private beach huts and be able to swim any time they choose without waiting in a queue? 'This system is all wrong,' said James to himself.

James could hear the sounds of people having fun in the sea. Grace's voice! And the silly 'Ha, ha, ha,' of Claud Sopworth.

He stopped walking and turned around to look at the long line of empty beach huts. The people who lived in Kimpton-on-Sea had a habit of giving their huts silly names. At this very moment, James was looking at Eagle's Nest, Buena Vista, and Mon Desir. As he was thinking about the names and whether they were suitable, he noticed that the door of Mon Desir was open.

It was only ten o'clock, too early for the rich and famous people of Kimpton-on-Sea to come down to swim.

'Pah! Not one of them will be down here before twelve o'clock,' thought James.

James looked up and down the beach; there were a lot of mothers with large families. They were too busy with their children to be watching him.

He looked again towards the sea. He heard Grace laugh again. It was followed by the 'Ha, ha, ha,' of Claud Sopworth.

'I'm doing it,' said James, moving quickly towards the open door before anyone could see him.

Once inside, he looked around. He saw some clothes hanging up, and for a moment he was worried. On the right-hand side, there was a girl's yellow jumper, an old beach hat and a pair of beach shoes. On the left-hand side, there was an old pair of grey trousers, a man's jumper, and a raincoat. But it was clear that there was no one around, so he decided to ignore the clothes, and quickly changed. Three minutes later, he was in the sea doing very short moments of professional-looking swimming.

'Oh, there you are!' cried Grace. 'I saw the crowds at the changing rooms and I was afraid you would be ages.'

James thought of the yellow book: *There are also times when it is better not to be quite so honest.*

'Really?' he replied to Grace.

At that moment he was happy again. He was able to say pleasantly to Claud Sopworth, who was teaching Grace to swim:

'No, no, you've got it all wrong. I'll show her.'

Claud moved away, leaving James to feel like the winner of their little competition.

Unfortunately, his moment of happiness didn't last very long. The temperature of the English sea doesn't make swimmers want to be in it for very long, and Grace and the Sopworth girls soon had blue chins. They raced up the beach together, and James had to go back on his own to Mon Desir.

As he pulled his shirt over his head, he was pleased with himself. He had, he felt, been dynamic.

Suddenly, he stood still in fear. He heard girls' voices outside – voices that were definitely not those of Grace and her friends. A moment later he realized the truth: the owners of Mon Desir were arriving.

It is possible that if James had been dressed, he would have waited there and attempted to explain. But he was not dressed, so instead he <u>panicked</u>. James grabbed the door and held it shut. Someone tried to pull it open from outside, but they were not successful.

'It's locked,' said a girl's voice. 'I thought Peg said it was open.'

'No, Woggle said so.'

'Oh, how annoying,' said the other girl. 'We'll have to go back for the key.'

James heard them walking away. He took a big breath – he was safe, at least for now.

In a hurry, he pulled on his clothes. Two minutes later he was walking slowly down the beach, trying to look <u>innocent</u>.

Grace and the Sopworths joined him on the beach a quarter of an hour later. At the end of the morning, Claud looked at his watch.

'It's lunchtime,' he said. 'We'd better go.'

'I'm so hungry,' said Alice.

All the other girls said that they were so hungry too.

'Are you coming, James?' asked Grace.

'Not if my clothes aren't good enough for you,' he said.

He waited for Grace to say that of course she wanted him to come with them, but the seaside air had changed her. She replied:

'Fine. See you this afternoon, then.'

'Well!' he said, watching the group walk away. 'Well, I can't...'

James couldn't think of anything else to say.

He walked slowly into the town, in a bad mood. There were two cafés in Kimpton-on-Sea; they were both hot, noisy and very busy. Just like at the changing rooms, James had to wait in a queue. At last he got a seat at a small table. He studied the menu with little interest, and thought to himself:

'Whatever I ask for, it's sure to not be available today. That's the kind of luck I have.'

His put his hands in his pockets. His right hand touched a strange object. It felt like a stone from the beach.

'When did I put a stone in my pocket?' thought James.

A waitress came up to him.

'Fried fish and potatoes, please,' said James.

'There's no fried fish left,' said the waitress, looking at the ceiling.

'Then I'll have beef curry,' said James.

'No beef curry either.'

'Is there anything on this awful menu that you do have?' demanded James.

The waitress pointed a pale-grey finger at one dull-sounding item on the menu. James ordered it.

He took his hand out of his pocket, bringing the stone with it. Opening his fingers, he looked at the object in his hand. The thing he held was not a stone; it was – he could hardly believe it – an emerald. *An enormous green emerald.*

James looked at it closely.

'No,' he thought, 'it couldn't be an emerald, it must be coloured glass. There couldn't be an emerald of that size. Unless...'

He saw the words from the newspaper in his mind: 'The Rajah of Maraputna – famous emerald the size of a small egg.' Was it— Could it really be *that* emerald he was looking at now?

The waitress returned with his food, and James hid the emerald in his hands.

He felt hot and cold at the same time. He didn't know what to do. If this was the emerald – *but was it? Could it be?* He opened his fingers to have another look. James was not an expert on jewels, but the colour of this one convinced him that it was real. He put both elbows on the table and looked down at the horrible food slowly going cold on the plate in front of him. He had to think. If this was the Rajah's emerald, what was he going to do about it?

The word 'police' came into his mind. If you found anything valuable, you took it to the police station.

Yes, but how had the emerald got into his trouser pocket? That was the question the police would ask. And at the moment he didn't have an answer to it.

How *had* the emerald got into his trouser pocket? He looked down at his legs. Something seemed wrong. He looked more closely. One pair of old grey trousers is very much like another pair of old grey trousers, but all the same, James suddenly had a feeling that these were not *his* old grey trousers.

He sat back in his chair, shocked. He saw now what had happened – in his hurry to get out of the beach hut, he had dressed himself in the wrong trousers. When he changed into his things for swimming, he remembered he had hung his own trousers next to the old pair already hanging there. So, that explained it – he had taken someone else's trousers.

But what was an emerald, worth hundreds and thousands of pounds, doing in an old pair of trousers in a beach hut? The more he thought about it, the stranger it seemed. He could, of course, explain everything to the police...

But, he would have to mention the fact that he had used a private beach hut. It wasn't a serious crime, but it was still embarrassing.

'Can I bring you anything else, sir?'

It was the waitress again. She was looking at his plate, which he hadn't yet touched. James asked for his bill. He paid and left.

As he stood in the street not sure what to do, he saw a newspaper in the shop opposite. It announced: *Rajah's emerald stolen.*

'Oh no,' said James, very quietly.

He found some money and bought a paper. He quickly found the story. _Burglar takes Famous Historical Emerald at Lord Edward Campion's. Rajah of Maraputna Very Upset._ The facts were simple. Lord Campion had had several friends at his house the evening before. The Rajah had gone to get the emerald to show to someone and had found it missing. The police had been called, but so far they had no idea who had taken it. James let the paper fall to the ground. It was still not clear to him how the emerald had come to be in the pocket of an old pair of trousers in a beach hut, but it was obvious now that the police would think that his story was suspicious. What should he do? All the police in Kimpton-on-Sea were busy searching for this jewel worth an enormous amount of money, and here he was, standing in the main street with it in his pocket.

He had two options. Option number one: go straight to the police station and tell his story – James wasn't sure about this.

Option number two: get rid of the emerald. He thought about sending it back to the Rajah by post. Then he shook his head – he had read too many detective stories for that sort of thing. He knew how a detective might be clever enough to discover the sender's profession, age, habits and personal appearance in no time at all. After that it would only be a couple of hours before they found him.

It was then that he had a wonderful and simple idea. It was lunchtime, and the beach was almost empty. He could return to Mon Desir, hang up the trousers where he had found them, and take his own instead. He started walking quickly back towards the beach huts.

As he walked, he began to feel guilty about his plan. The emerald should be returned to the Rajah. He thought that maybe he could do some detective work himself, to help get the emerald back to its owner – he would start by finding out who owned Mon Desir. So, he went to talk to the old man at the changing rooms.

'Excuse me!' said James politely; 'but I believe a friend of mine has a hut on this beach, Mr Charles Lampton. I think it's called Mon Desir.'

The old man was looking out to sea. He replied without moving his eyes away from the view:

'No, Mon Desir belongs to Lord Campion. Everyone knows that. I've never heard of Mr Charles Lampton – he must be new.'

'Thank you,' said James.

The information confused him. Had the Rajah put the stone into the pocket himself and forgotten it? No, that seemed very unlikely to James. So one of the other house-guests must be the thief. The situation reminded James of some of his favourite fiction.

Anyway, he still had his plan. When he arrived, the door of Mon Desir was still open. No one saw him go in. James was just getting his own trousers when a voice behind him made him turn round suddenly.

'So I've caught you, my man!' said the stranger, a well-dressed man of about forty. 'I've caught you!' he repeated.

'Who – who are you?' asked James.

'I'm Detective-Inspector Merrilees from the Kimpton police,' said the man. 'And I must ask you to hand over that emerald.'

'The – the emerald?'

James tried to think.

'I – I don't know what you're talking about,' he said.

'Oh, yes, my boy, I think you do.'

James quickly changed his plan.

'Listen, this whole thing's a mistake,' he said. 'I can explain it quite easily—'

'Yes, they all say that,' said the policeman. 'I suppose you picked it up when you were walking along the beach, eh?'

James's story was actually a bit like that... So he tried to <u>buy time</u> to allow himself to make a new plan.

'How do I know you are who you say you are?' he demanded.

Merrilees opened his coat for a moment, to show a small silver <u>badge</u> in his inside pocket.

'This is my police badge,' he said.

James couldn't believe what he was seeing.

Then Merrilees smiled and said, in an almost friendly voice, 'This is the first time you've stolen something, isn't it?'

James found he couldn't speak, so he <u>nodded</u>.

'Mmmm, I thought so. Now, my boy, are you going to give me that emerald?'

James found his voice.

'I— I haven't got it with me.' He was thinking quickly.

'Left it at your boarding house?' asked Merrilees. James nodded again.

'Okay, then,' said the detective, 'we'll go there together.'

He put his arm through James's.

'I'm taking no chances – you won't escape from me,' he said gently.

James spoke in a nervous voice.

'If I do, will you let me go?' he asked.

Merrilees appeared to be embarrassed.

'That's up to the Rajah, of course,' he explained. 'But you know what these foreign kings are like.'

James, who knew nothing about foreign kings, and was very confused, nodded his head.

'It's not what usually happens, of course,' said the detective; 'but you may <u>get off</u> with it.'

Again James nodded. They had walked all the way along the beach, and were now turning into the town.

Suddenly James paused and half-spoke. Merrilees looked up quickly, and then laughed. They were just passing the police station, and he noticed James was nervous.

'I'm giving you a chance first,' he said smiling.

It was at that moment that things began to happen. James grabbed the other man's arm, and shouted: 'Help! Thief! Help! Thief!'

A crowd surrounded them in less than a minute. Merrilees was trying to get his arm away from James.

'Arrest this man,' cried James. 'Arrest this man, he stole something out of my pocket.'

'What are you talking about, you fool?' cried Merrilees. A policeman appeared. Mr Merrilees and James were taken into the police station. James repeated what he had said.

'This man has just stolen something out of my pocket. He's got my wallet in his right-hand pocket, there!'

'The man is mad,' said Merrilees. 'You can look for yourself and see if he is telling the truth.'

The policeman put his hand into Merrilees's pocket. He took something out.

'What's this?' said the policeman, shocked. 'It must be the Rajah's emerald!'

Merrilees looked more shocked than anyone else. 'This is impossible.' He could hardly get his words out. 'Impossible! The man must have put it into my pocket himself as we were walking along together.'

The policeman wasn't sure who to believe. Now he was suspicious of James, too. He said something quietly to another policeman, who left the room.

'Now then,' said the policeman, 'tell me what happened please, one at a time.'

'Certainly,' said James. 'I was walking along the beach, when I met this man, and he <u>pretended</u> he knew me. I couldn't remember having met him before, but I was too polite to say so. We walked along together. I was a bit suspicious of him, and just when we got opposite the police station, I found his hand in my pocket. I held on to him and shouted for help.'

The policeman turned to Merrilees. 'And now you, sir.'

Merrilees seemed a little embarrassed.

'The story is very nearly right,' he said slowly; 'but not quite. I didn't pretend to know this man – it was him who pretended to know me. I suppose he was trying to get rid of the emerald, and put it into my pocket while we were talking.'

The policeman stopped writing.

'Ah!' he said. 'Well, there'll be a man here in a minute who'll help us to get to the truth of the case.'

Merrilees looked annoyed.

'I really can't wait,' he said, looking at his watch. 'I have an appointment. You can't really believe I'd steal the emerald and then walk along with it in my pocket?'

'It isn't likely, sir, I agree,' the policeman replied. 'But you'll have to wait five or ten minutes. Ah! Here's Lord Campion now.'

A tall man of forty walked into the room. He was wearing a pair of old trousers and an old jumper.

'What's going on?' he asked. 'You've got the emerald, I hear? That's excellent, well done. Who are these people?'

His eyes looked quickly over James and then at Merrilees. Merrilees seemed to grow smaller.

'Jones!' cried Lord Campion.

'You recognize this man, Lord Campion?' asked the policeman.

'Of course I do,' he replied. 'He's my driver – he started a month ago. Is he involved in this? The policeman they sent down from London was immediately suspicious of him, but the emerald wasn't anywhere in his room.'

'He was carrying it in his coat pocket, sir,' the policeman explained. He pointed to James. 'This man told us about him.'

'My dear boy, thank you,' said Lord Campion. 'So you were suspicious of him all along, you say?'

'Yes,' said James. 'I had to <u>make up</u> the story about him stealing from my pocket to get him into the police station.'

'Well, it's excellent,' said Lord Campion, 'absolutely excellent. You must come back and have lunch with us. The Rajah will want to thank you for returning his emerald to him. I don't quite understand the story yet, but you can explain it again.'

They were outside the police station by now, standing on the steps.

'Actually,' said James, 'I'd like to tell you the true story.'

So he did. Lord Campion was very entertained.

'That's the best thing I've heard in my whole life,' he said, laughing. 'I understand it all now. Jones must have known the police would look for the emerald in the house, so he took it down to the beach hut as soon as he had stolen it. He also knew that nobody would touch that old pair of trousers I sometimes put on for fishing, and he could collect the jewel any time he wanted. It must have been a shock to him when he went there today and it was gone. When you appeared, he realized that it was you who had removed the jewel. I still don't understand how you knew he wasn't a real detective, though!'

James thought to himself: *A strong man does not always say everything he knows.*

He just smiled, as he gently passed his fingers over the inside of his coat, feeling the little silver badge he was wearing on his inside pocket. It was from a small club, the Merton Park Super Cycling Club. And it was exactly the same as the badge that Merrilees, or Jones, had shown him to prove that he was a policeman! He had recognized it immediately.

'Hello, James!'

He turned. Grace and the Sopworth girls were calling to him from the other side of the road. He turned to Lord Campion.

'Will you excuse me a moment?'

He crossed the road to them.

'We're going to the cinema,' said Grace. 'We thought you might like to come.'

'I'm sorry,' said James. 'I'm just on my way to have lunch with Lord Edward Campion. Yes, that man over there in the comfortable old clothes. He wants me to meet the Rajah of Maraputna.'

With that, he left them.

# Philomel Cottage

◆ ◆ ◆

Alix Martin stood at the garden gate, watching her husband walk down the road towards the village.

Alix knew she was not beautiful. She had had a difficult life. Her mother had always been unwell, so when Alix was eighteen she had had to get a job in an office to earn money for them both. She had been very <u>business-like</u> and efficient for a very long time. But now, her face was relaxed and happy – her old colleagues would hardly recognize her.

There had been one romance back then. His name was Dick Windyford. To everyone else, it looked as though they were only friends but Alix knew it was more than that. Dick had very little money – he had to pay for his younger brother to go to school and this took most of his salary. So, for the moment, he could not think about marriage.

And then suddenly everything in Alix's life had changed. A cousin she didn't know had died and Alix was given his money. It meant Alix didn't have to work any more – and it meant she and Dick could finally get married.

Alix expected Dick to be excited at this news, but he wasn't. He seemed depressed, and he avoided her. Alix quickly realized the truth. She had become an independent woman, and Dick was too <u>proud</u> to ask her to be his wife.

She liked him for this, and was wondering whether she should ask him to marry her, when for the second time something unexpected happened.

She met Gerald Martin at a friend's house. Alix, in total surprise, had fallen quickly in love, and within a week they were engaged.

Without meaning to, Alix had found the way to make Dick want her.

'The man's a stranger!' Dick said, angry. 'You don't know anything about him!'

'I know that I love him.'

'How can you know – in a week?'

'It doesn't take everyone eleven years to find out that they're in love with a girl,' replied Alix, angrily.

His face went white.

'I've cared about you ever since I met you. I thought that you cared about me too.'

Alix was honest.

'I thought so, too,' she admitted. 'But that was because I didn't know what love was.'

Then Dick had <u>begged</u> her to stay with him. When that didn't work he had said he would hurt Gerald. Alix was surprised to see such strong feelings in the man she thought she had known so well.

Now, standing at her garden gate on this sunny morning, she thought back to that conversation. She had been married for a month, and she was wonderfully happy. Yet, with her husband gone for the moment, she felt a little anxious suddenly. And the reason she felt anxious was Dick Windyford.

Since her marriage she had had the same dream three times. In the dream, she saw her husband lying dead, and Dick standing over him, and she knew without doubt that Dick had killed him.

This was horrible enough, but there was something more horrible still. In her dream, Alix Martin was glad that her husband was dead; *she thanked the murderer!* Then the dream always ended the same way, with her in Dick Windyford's arms.

She hadn't said anything about this dream to her husband, but it had upset her a lot. Was it a warning about Dick?

Alix's thoughts were interrupted by the ringing of the telephone from inside the house. She entered the cottage and answered it. Suddenly she swayed, and put a hand against the wall.

She asked, 'Who did you say was speaking?'

'Alix, what's the matter with your voice? I wouldn't have recognized it – you sound different. It's Dick.'

'Oh!' said Alix. 'Oh! Where— where are you?'

'At the village pub near you – the Traveller's Arms, I think? I'm on holiday. Do you mind me coming to your house to say hello to you both this evening after dinner?'

'No!' said Alix quickly. 'You can't come!'

Dick paused before he spoke again. His voice sounded different now.

'I apologize for asking,' he said, in a serious voice. 'Of course I won't come—'

Alix was embarrassed.

'I only meant that… we're busy tonight,' she explained, trying to make her voice sound as natural as possible. 'Will you— will you come for dinner tomorrow night instead?'

But Dick clearly noticed that her voice didn't sound as friendly as her words.

'Thanks very much,' he said, in the same formal voice as before, 'but I may leave soon. It depends if a friend of mine arrives or not. Goodbye, Alix.' He paused, and then added quickly, in a more friendly voice: 'Good luck, my dear.'

Alix hung up the phone.

'He can't come here,' she repeated to herself. 'He can't. Oh, what a fool I am! It's just a dream... I'm still glad he isn't coming, though.'

She picked up a hat from the table, and went out into the garden again. She stopped to look up at the name of the house above the door: Philomel[4] Cottage.

'Isn't it a very silly name?' she had said to Gerald when they moved in.

'You little Cockney[5],' he had said, laughing. 'I suppose you've never heard a <u>nightingale</u> sing, have you? Well, I'm glad you haven't. Nightingales should sing only for people in love[4]. We can listen to them together on a summer's evening.'

It was Gerald who had found Philomel Cottage. He had been so excited to tell her that he had found the perfect house for them to rent. And when Alix had seen it she had loved it too. It was true that the house was rather lonely – they were two miles from the nearest village – but the cottage itself was so beautiful. It was perfectly traditional and she fell in love with it immediately. But then there was a problem. The owner suddenly decided not to rent out the cottage – he wanted to sell it instead.

Although Gerald had money, it was all in <u>investments</u> so he couldn't use it. The owner was asking for three thousand pounds. Gerald had only one thousand pounds. But Alix really wanted to live in Philomel Cottage. They decided she would use her cousin's money to buy their home. So Philomel Cottage became theirs, and Alix had never regretted it since. She had worked all her adult life, but now enjoyed cooking meals for Gerald and looking after the house instead.

The garden, however, was looked after by a gardener from the village, who came twice a week.

As she came round the side of the house, Alix was surprised to see the old gardener busy planting flowers. She was surprised because his days for work were Mondays and Fridays, and today was Wednesday.

'George, what are you doing here?' she asked.

The old man laughed.

'I thought you'd be surprised. But there's a village <u>fête</u> on Friday, and I said to myself, Mr Martin and his lovely wife won't mind if I come on Wednesday instead of Friday just this once.'

'Of course,' said Alix. 'I hope you enjoy yourself at the fête.'

'I plan to,' said George. 'I also thought, Mrs Martin, that I would be able to see you before you go away, so you can tell me what you want me to do with the garden while you're away. You're not sure yet when you'll be back, is that right?'

'I'm not going away!' Alix was confused.

George looked at her, also confused.

'Aren't you going to London tomorrow?' he asked.

'No. What put that idea into your head?' asked Alix.

George pointed down the road.

'I met Mr Gerald in the village yesterday. He told me you were both going away to London tomorrow, and he didn't know when you'd be back again.'

'How strange,' said Alix, laughing. 'You mustn't have understood him.'

She wondered exactly what it was that Gerald had said to make the old man think that. The two of them going to London? She never wanted to go to London again.

'I hate London,' she said suddenly.

'Ah!' said George. 'I must be wrong. But it's strange... He said it very clearly. Anyway, I'm glad you're staying here. It's good to stay in one place, and I don't like London either. Too many cars – that's the problem nowadays. Once people have got a car, they can't stay still anywhere. Mr Ames, who used to have this house, was a nice peaceful man until he bought one of those things. He'd only had it a month and suddenly he decided to sell this cottage. And he'd spent a lot of money on it too, with sinks in all the bedrooms, and electric lights[6] and everything else. "You'll never get your money back," I said to him. "But," he said to me, "I know I can get two thousand pounds for this house." And he was right – he did.'

'He got three thousand pounds,' said Alix, smiling.

'Two thousand,' repeated George.

'It really was three thousand,' said Alix.

'Ladies never understand money,' said George. 'You're not telling me that Mr Ames asked you for three thousand pounds?'

'He didn't ask me,' said Alix; 'he asked my husband.'

George turned away from Alix, back to his work.

'The price was two thousand,' he said again.

Alix didn't want to argue with him. She moved away and began to pick some flowers.

As she moved back towards the house with her flowers, Alix noticed a small, dark-green object sitting between some leaves in one of the plants. It was her husband's diary.

She opened it, reading some of the pages with a smile. Almost from the beginning of their married life she had realized that although Gerald could be <u>impulsive</u> and <u>emotional,</u> he could also be very efficient. He liked his meals at the exact same time each day, and he always planned his day carefully.

Looking through the diary, it made her laugh when she read what he had written for May 14th: *Marry Alix, St Peter's 2.30pm*

'The big silly,' Alix said to herself, turning the pages. When she reached today's date, she stopped.

*Wednesday, June 18<sup>th</sup>*

In the space for that day, Gerald had written in his neat writing: *9 pm*

Nothing else.

*What did Gerald plan to do at 9 pm?* Alix wondered. She smiled to herself as she realized that, had this been a story, like those she so often read, the diary would probably have had the name of another woman in it. She looked at the pages at the back of the book. There were dates, appointments, some notes about business, but only one woman's name – her own.

Yet as she put the book into her pocket and went into the house with her flowers, she felt worried. Dick's words came back to her, so clearly it felt like he was standing next to her: 'The man's a stranger. You don't know anything about him.'

It was true. What did she know about him? After all, Gerald was forty. In forty years there must have been important people in his life before her...

Alix was annoyed with herself. These were silly thoughts. She had something more important to think about. Should she, or should she not, tell her husband that Dick Windyford had called her?

It was possible that Gerald had already seen Dick in the village. Then he would probably tell her about it as soon as he got home. Otherwise – what? Alix had a feeling that she shouldn't tell him that Dick was here.

If she told him, he would suggest inviting Dick to dinner. Then she would have to explain that Dick had already suggested that, and that she had made an excuse to stop him from coming. And when he asked her why she had done that, what could she say?

Could she tell him about her dream? He would laugh, she was sure. And she felt so serious about this dream, she didn't want him to laugh.

Alix decided not to say anything. It was the first secret she had ever kept from her husband, and it made her feel bad.

When she heard Gerald come back just before lunch, she hurried into the kitchen and <u>pretended</u> to be busy cooking.

It was obvious that Gerald had not seen Dick in the village. Alix decided – she was definitely not going to tell him.

Alix didn't remember the diary until after their evening meal. They were in the sitting room with the windows open to let in the sweet smell of the flowers from the garden.

'Here's something I found today in the garden,' she said, and threw it to him. 'I know all your secrets now.'

'Not <u>guilty</u>,' said Gerald, smiling.

'What about your secret meeting at nine o'clock tonight?'

'Oh! That...' He seemed shocked for a moment; then he smiled rather <u>strangely</u>. 'It's a secret meeting with a very nice girl. She's got brown hair and blue eyes, and she's very like you.'

'I don't understand,' said Alix, pretending to be angry. 'Tell me what you mean.'

'OK. That's to remind me to <u>develop</u> some photographs tonight, and I want you to help me.'

Gerald liked taking photographs. He had an old-fashioned camera, and he developed his own photographs in their <u>cellar</u>.

'And it must be done at nine o'clock,' said Alix with a smile.

Gerald looked a little annoyed.

'My dear,' he said, 'people should always plan things for a definite time. Then you complete all your work properly.'

Alix sat for a minute or two in silence, watching her husband as he relaxed in his chair, smoking. Suddenly, she panicked and cried out before she could stop herself, 'Oh, Gerald, I wish I knew more about you!'

Her husband looked at her in surprise.

'But, my dear Alix, you do know all about me. I've told you about my childhood in Northumberland, about my life in South Africa, and about these last ten years in Canada where I was successful.'

'But that's all business!' said Alix.

Gerald laughed suddenly.

'You women are all the same. You're only interested in love.'

Alix's throat felt dry. 'Well... But there must have been some women...?'

There was silence again for a moment or two. Gerald was thinking hard. When he spoke, he spoke seriously.

'Do you think it's a good idea, Alix – these questions? There have been women in my life; yes, of course there have. You wouldn't believe me if I said there hadn't been. But honestly, not one of them meant anything to me.'

Alix believed him.

'Are you satisfied?' he asked, with a smile. Gerald was curious. 'What has made you think about this tonight?'

Alix got up, and began to walk about.

'Oh, I don't know,' she said. 'I've been upset all day.'

'That's strange,' said Gerald, in a quiet voice, as though he was speaking to himself. 'That's very strange.'

'Why is it strange?'

'Oh, my lovely girl, don't be angry with me. I only said it was strange because usually you're so sweet and calm.'

Alix tried to smile.

'Everything's annoyed me today,' she said. 'Even old George the gardener had some stupid idea that we were going away to London. He said you had told him so.'

'Where did you see him?' asked Gerald quickly.

'He came to work today instead of Friday,' she explained.

'Old fool,' said Gerald angrily.

Alix was surprised. She had never seen her husband so angry. Seeing the look on Alix's face, Gerald tried to control himself.

'Well, he *is* an old fool,' he repeated.

'What did you say to make him think that we were going away?' Alix asked him.

'Me? I never said anything. At least—Oh, yes, I remember; I made some silly joke about going "off to London in the morning," and I suppose he thought I was serious. Or maybe he didn't hear me properly. You told him we weren't going, didn't you?'

He waited for her to reply, looking anxious.

'Of course, but once he gets an idea in his head – well, it isn't so easy to get it out again.'

Then she told him what George had said about the price of the cottage.

Gerald was silent for a minute or two, then he said slowly:

'I gave Mr Ames two thousand pounds in cash and the one thousand through a <u>mortgage</u>. That's probably why George was confused.'

'Probably,' said Alix.

Then she looked up at the clock, and said with a smile.

'We should go and do those photographs, Gerald. We're five minutes late already.'

Gerald smiled strangely. 'I've changed my mind,' he said quietly; 'I don't want to do any photography tonight.'

When she went to bed that Wednesday night, Alix's mind was peaceful and she felt happy again.

But by the evening of the next day she realized that something was still worrying her. Dick had not called again, but his words were still in her head: "The man's a stranger. You don't know anything about him." And then she remembered the look on her husband's face when he said, "Do you think it's a good idea, Alix – these questions?" *Why had he said that?*

It had been a warning. It meant: 'You had better not look for my secrets, Alix. You may not like what you find.'

By Friday morning, Alix was sure that there had been a woman in Gerald's life – someone that he didn't want her to know about. She was jealous.

Was his story about developing photographs a lie? Had he been planning to meet a woman that night at 9 pm?

Three days ago she had thought that she knew her husband. Now it seemed that he was a stranger. She remembered how angry he had been about old George. A small thing, perhaps, but it showed her that she didn't really know the man who was her husband.

That afternoon, Alix suggested that she should go to the village to get some things they needed. She was surprised when Gerald insisted on going instead while she stayed at home. Why was he so anxious to stop her going to the village?

Suddenly, she had a thought that explained everything. Was it possible that, without saying anything to her, Gerald *had* seen Dick? Was Gerald also jealous? Did he want to prevent her from seeing Dick again? To Alix, this explanation seemed to match the facts.

Yet after tea-time she was worried again. There was something she knew she had to do. Pretending to herself that the room needed cleaning, she went upstairs to look in her husband's things.

She needed to be sure.

Feeling guilty, she searched through packets of letters and documents, opened drawers, and even looked in the pockets of her husband's clothes. There was one drawer that was locked. Alix was now certain that she would find something about this woman of the past in that drawer.

She remembered that Gerald had left his keys downstairs. She fetched them and tried each one. She was annoyed when none of the keys fitted the final drawer. Alix needed to know what was in it. So, she went into the other rooms and brought back all the keys she could find.

She was lucky – the key for the wardrobe in the spare room also fitted the drawer. She pulled it open quickly – but there was nothing in it except for some old newspaper articles.

Alix wondered what had interested Gerald so much that he had kept the articles. They were nearly all American papers from seven years ago. They were about the well-known <u>swindler</u> and <u>bigamist</u> Charles Lemaitre. It was believed that Lemaitre had killed a number of women. Human bones had been found under the floor of one of the houses he had rented, and most of the women he had 'married' had disappeared.

He had cleverly defended himself and was found *not guilty* of murder, but he was put in prison for swindling and bigamy.

Alix remembered the case clearly – including the fact that Lemaitre had escaped from prison three years later. She remembered how the newspapers had talked about how charming he had been in <u>court</u>. She also remembered that they had said he had a weak heart.

There was a photo of Charles Lemaitre in one of the articles. Alix studied it – he had a long beard and looked intelligent.

The face reminded her of someone. *Who was it?* Suddenly, with a shock, she realized that it was Gerald – the eyes were the same. Perhaps that's why he had kept the articles. She began to read the paragraph next to the photograph. It said that Lemaitre had written the dates when he had killed the women in his diary. It also said that the prisoner could be recognized by a <u>mole</u> near the bottom of his left arm.

Alix dropped the papers and swayed. On the bottom of his left arm, her husband had a small <u>scar</u>...

The room moved around her. *Gerald Martin was Charles Lemaitre!* She knew it. It was like the pieces of a puzzle fitting together.

He had used only her money to pay two thousand pounds for the house; there was no mortgage. Even the meaning of her dream became obvious now. Her <u>subconscious</u> mind had always been afraid of Gerald Martin and wanted to escape from him. And it was Dick Windyford who saved her.

It was easy now to see the truth. She was Lemaitre's next woman. And he would kill her soon. Very soon, perhaps...

With a cry, she remembered something. Wednesday, 9pm. His plan for them to develop photographs in the cellar. He had buried one of his women in a cellar before. So it had been all planned for Wednesday night. But to write it down in his diary – that was crazy! Or was it? Gerald always wrote all his plans and meetings down; murder was like any other business meeting to him.

But what had saved her? What could possibly have saved her? Had Gerald felt bad at the last minute? No. Suddenly, the answer came to her – old George.

She understood now why her husband had been so angry. He must have told everyone that they were going to London the next day. Then George had come to work in the garden on the wrong day, he had mentioned London to her, and she had told him they weren't going anywhere. It would have been too dangerous to kill her that night in case old George repeated that conversation to anyone. How lucky she had been! If she hadn't mentioned that unimportant conversation with George to Gerald... Alix suddenly felt scared.

And then she heard the garden gate.

For a moment Alix couldn't move, then she walked quietly to the window, and looked out from behind the curtain.

Yes, it was her husband. He was smiling and singing. In his hand he had an object which almost made Alix's heart stop. It was a new spade. He was going to kill her tonight.

But there was still a chance. Gerald was going round to the back of the house.

Alix ran down the stairs and out of the front door. But just as she came out of the door, her husband came round the other side of the house.

'Hello,' he said, 'where are you going in such a hurry?'

Alix tried to appear calm and normal.

'Oh, I was just going to walk to the end of the road and back,' she said in a voice that didn't sound like hers.

'OK,' said Gerald. 'I'll come with you.'

'No – please, Gerald. I've got a headache – I'd rather go alone.'

He looked at her. Was he suspicious?

'What's the matter, Alix? You're pale.'

'Nothing.' She tried to smile. 'I've got a headache, that's all. A walk will make me feel better.'

Gerald laughed easily. 'Well, I'm coming, whether you want me to or not.'

She couldn't say no. If he thought that she knew...

Alix tried hard to behave normally, yet she was worried that he knew something was wrong.

When they returned to the house he insisted that she lie down. He was, as always, the perfect husband. Alix felt caught.

He wouldn't leave her alone for even a minute. He stayed in the kitchen with her while she prepared dinner. Then they sat down together to eat.

It was hard for Alix to eat the meal. It was even harder to have a conversation with Gerald. She knew her life was in danger. She was alone with this man, with no one nearby to help her.

She tried to think what she could do. Could she tell him that Dick was coming to see them that evening?

No, that wouldn't work. This man would not put it off a second time. If she told him *anything* about Dick, it might make him kill her sooner. He would murder her there and then, and calmly call Dick with a story about how they had had to go away. Oh, if only Dick was coming to the house this evening!

Suddenly, she had an idea. She felt brave.

She made coffee and took it out to the garden, where they often sat on fine evenings.

'By the way,' said Gerald suddenly, 'we'll develop those photographs later.'

Alix was scared but she replied, 'Can't you manage alone? I'm rather tired tonight.'

'Oh, it won't take long.' He smiled to himself. 'And I promise, you won't be tired afterwards.'

He smiled. Carefully smiling back at him, Alix knew that her plan had to happen *now,* or it would be too late.

She stood up.

'I'm just going to telephone the butcher,' she said.

'The butcher? At this time of night?'

'His shop's shut, of course, silly. But he's at home. And I need some meat for tomorrow.'

She went into the house and closed the door behind her. She heard Gerald say, 'Don't shut the door.'

She replied quickly, 'It keeps the insects out. I hate insects. Are you afraid that I like the butcher, silly?'

When she was inside the house, she grabbed the telephone and called the Traveller's Arms.

'Is Mr Dick Windyford still there? Can I speak to him?'

Then she felt sick. The door was pushed open and her husband came in.

'Go away, Gerald,' she said. 'I hate anyone listening when I'm talking on the telephone.'

He laughed and sat down. 'Are you sure it really is the butcher you're calling?'

Alix didn't know what to do. Her plan had not worked. In a minute Dick Windyford would come to the phone. Should she cry out to him for help?

As she was thinking about this, she realized she was pressing the little <u>mute</u> key on the telephone she was holding. Suddenly she had another plan, but it wasn't going to be easy.

'It means staying calm,' she thought to herself. 'and thinking of the right words to say. I believe I can do it. I *must* do it.'

And at that moment she heard Dick Windyford's voice at the other end of the phone.

Alix took a slow breath in. '*Hello, this is Mrs Martin from Philomel Cottage. Please come* (she pressed mute so that Dick could not hear her now) *tomorrow morning with two nice steaks* (she pressed mute off again). *It's very important* (mute on). Thank you so much, Mr Hexworthy: I hope you don't mind me calling you so late, but those steaks are really (mute off) *a matter of life or death* (mute on). OK – tomorrow morning (mute off) *as early as possible, please. Goodbye.*'

She put the phone down and turned to her husband.

'So that's how you talk to your butcher, is it?' said Gerald.

'Yes, that's how I get what I want,' said Alix.

She was excited now. He wasn't at all suspicious. Dick might not completely understand the message, but she was sure he would come anyway.

She went into the sitting room. Gerald followed her.

'You seem happier now,' he said, watching her closely.

'Yes,' said Alix. 'My headache's gone.'

She sat down and smiled at her husband as he sat in the chair opposite her. She was saved. It was only twenty-five minutes past eight. Dick would be here before nine o'clock.

'I didn't like that coffee you gave me very much,' complained Gerald. 'It tasted very bitter.'

'It's a different kind. That's fine, we won't have it again if you don't like it.'

Alix started to sew. Gerald read a few pages of his book. Then he glanced up at the clock and threw the book down.

'It's half-past eight. Time to go down to the cellar.'

The dress Alix was sewing slipped from her fingers.

'Oh, not yet. Let's wait until nine o'clock.'

'No, my dear – half-past eight. That's the time in my diary.'

'But I'd rather wait until nine – I'm busy.'

'You know when I say a time I always mean it, Alix. Let's go.'

Alix looked up at him and was afraid. Gerald looked excited. Alix thought, 'It's true – he can't wait to kill me.'

He came over to her, and pulled her onto her feet.

'Come on – or I'll carry you there.'

His voice scared her. She pulled herself away from him. She was very frightened now. She couldn't escape.

'Now, Alix—'

'No! No! Gerald, stop – I've got something to tell you. I've done something.'

He stopped.

'You've done something?' he said, curious now.

'Yes.' She had said the words without thinking, but now she knew she had to keep his attention.

'This is about a former boyfriend, I suppose,' he said in a nasty voice.

'No,' said Alix. 'Something else. I suppose you'd call it a... crime.'

Immediately she saw that he was interested. She began to feel braver.

'You'd better sit down again,' she said quietly.

She tried to look calm, but inside she was making up a story as quickly as she could. Her story had to <u>buy her time</u> until help arrived.

'I told you,' she said slowly, 'that I had worked in an office for fifteen years. That wasn't completely true. When I was twenty-two I met an elderly man who had some investments. He fell in love with me and asked me to marry him. I accepted and we got married.' She paused.

Her husband was suddenly interested, and she continued. 'Do you know anything about <u>poison</u>?'

She knew that if he did, she would have to be very careful with what she said next. She stopped breathing for a moment.

'No,' said Gerald, 'I know very little about them.'

Alix breathed out. 'There is one poison which is a white powder. A very small amount can kill someone. It makes the death look like a heart attack.'

She paused. 'Go on,' said Gerald.

'No. I'm afraid. I can't tell you. Another time.'

'Tell me now,' he said, annoyed. 'I want to know.'

'Well... We'd been married a month. I was very good to my elderly husband – I was very kind. Everyone knew what a good wife I was. But one evening, when we were alone together, I put some of the poison in his usual cup of coffee...'

Alix paused.

'It was very peaceful. I sat watching him. Once he asked for air, so I opened the window. Then he said he couldn't move from his chair. A few minutes later, he died.'

She stopped, smiling.

'*Hurry up, Dick,*' she thought.

She continued, trying to keep Gerald interested: 'Then I went back to my office job, and I met another man. He didn't know I'd been married before. He was a younger man, rather good-looking, and quite rich. We got married in Sussex. He liked me to make coffee for him in the evening, too.'

Alix smiled again, and added, 'I make very good coffee.'

Then she continued:

'My second husband died very suddenly from a heart attack one evening after dinner. I didn't like the doctor. I don't think he was suspicious of me, but he was very surprised at my young husband's death.

'I don't know why I went back to the office after that – I didn't need to. I got about four thousand pounds from my second husband. Then, you see—'

But she was interrupted. Gerald, his face red, unable to breathe properly, was pointing a finger at her.

'The coffee... the coffee! I understand now why it was bitter. You've done it again. You've put poison in *my* coffee!'

He was so angry that Alix was scared. She was worried he was going to attack her. She was about to tell him it wasn't true, but then she paused. She looked into his eyes.

'Yes,' she said. 'I put poison in your coffee too. Already the poison is working. At this moment you can't move from your chair – you can't move at all.'

If she could keep him there – even for a few minutes...

*What was that?* She heard the sound of the gate opening.

Then the front door.

'You can't move,' she said again.

Then she ran past him out of the room and fell into Dick's arms, crying.

'Alix?' he cried, worried.

Then he turned to the man with him, a tall man in a police uniform.

'Go and see what's been happening in that room.

'My dear,' he said quietly to Alix. 'My poor dear girl. What's he done to you?'

The policeman came back.

'There's only a man sitting in a chair. He looks as though he's been very frightened, and... Well, he's dead.'

Suddenly Alix spoke. She spoke as though she was dreaming, her eyes closed.

'And then,' she said, almost as though she were reading from a story, 'he died...'

# The Actress

◆ ◆ ◆

The <u>shabby</u> man in the fourth row of the theatre sat forward and looked up at the stage. Jake Levitt couldn't believe what he was seeing.

'Nancy Taylor!' he said quietly to himself. 'Little Nancy Taylor!'

He glanced at the show information he was holding in his hand. One name was a little larger than the rest.

'Olga Stormer. So that's what you're calling yourself now. You think you're a big, famous star, don't you? And you must be making a lot of money too. You've probably forgotten your name was ever Nancy Taylor. I wonder what you'd say if I reminded you...'

The play ended. The audience clapped loudly. Olga Stormer, the great actress, was brilliant yet again.

Jake did not join in the clapping, but there was a smile on his face.

How lucky he felt! He really needed some money, and he thought that Olga might be the person to give him some. He supposed that she would try to say it wasn't true, but *he* knew the truth. If he could make his idea work, he was sure he could get lots and lots of money from her...

◆ ◆ ◆

The next morning, Olga Stormer received a letter. She stood in her beautiful room at the back of the theatre and read it several times. She thought carefully for a while. Her pale face, which had the ability to show so many different feelings, now showed no feelings at all. When she had finished reading, her grey-green eyes looked out far in front of her at something that wasn't there, like she could see the danger standing in front of her.

In that wonderful voice of hers, Olga called: 'Miss Jones!'

A neat young woman with glasses came quickly into the room.

'Phone Mr Danahan, please, and ask him to come here, immediately.'

Syd Danahan, Olga Stormer's manager, entered the room, looking worried as usual. His job changed daily depending on Olga's mood. Sometimes his job was to encourage Olga to do something, and sometimes it was to persuade her not to do something; sometimes it was to *make* her do something, and sometimes it was all these things at the same time. Today, he was pleased to see that Olga seemed calm. She pushed a letter across the table to him.

'Read that.'

The letter was written badly, on cheap paper.

*Dear Miss Stormer,*
*I enjoyed your theatre performance last night. I believe that we both know Miss Nancy Taylor. An article about her is going to be published very soon. If you would like to discuss this article with me, I could visit you at any time.*
*Yours,*
*Jake Levitt*

Danahan looked confused.

'I don't understand. Who's Nancy Taylor?'

'A girl who I thought was dead, Danny.' Her voice sounded strange and tired. It made her seem older than her thirty-four years. 'A girl who *was* dead until this <u>carrion crow</u> brought her to life again.'

'Oh! Then...'

'It's me, Danny. I'm Nancy Taylor.'

'Ah. And this man wants money to keep quiet?'

She <u>nodded</u>. 'And he knows what to say to get it.'

Danahan looked serious as he thought about everything he had just discovered.

'What about lying? You can say that he's wrong – that you just look like Nancy.'

Olga shook her head.

'Levitt makes his money this way. He knows what he's doing. He knows he's right.'

'What about the police?' Danahan asked.

Her small smile told him that the answer was no. Although Danahan didn't realize it, Olga's quick brain was waiting for his slower brain to reach the same conclusions that she had.

'Maybe you should – er – say something to Sir[3] Richard? That would stop this man, wouldn't it?'

The actress was going to marry Sir Richard Everard, MP[7]. It had been announced a few weeks before.

'Oh, I told Richard everything when he asked me to marry him. But it doesn't make any difference – if this man Levitt does what he says he's going to do then that will be the end of my career, and of Richard's career, too[7]. No, I think there are only two options.'

'Yes?'

'To pay – and that, of course, will never stop. Or to disappear and start again.'

She sounded tired again.

'I don't regret what I did, Danny. I was a poor, hungry girl trying hard to make a good life for myself.' She stopped, seemed to think for a moment, then continued: 'But I shot a man – a horrible man who deserved to be shot. After what he did to me, no <u>jury</u> on earth would have found me <u>guilty</u> of murder. I know that now, but at the time I was a frightened kid and... I ran.'

Danahan nodded.

'Well,' he said, 'Maybe we could find out something that Levitt is guilty of too – and use it to keep him quiet.'

Olga shook her head.

'He's a <u>coward</u> – he won't have done anything very bad.'

She paused...

'A coward!' she repeated. 'I wonder...'

'What about if Sir Richard went to see him and frightened him?' suggested Danahan.

'No, Richard is too nice. You can't deal with a man like Levitt by being nice.'

'Well, let me see him, then.'

'Excuse me, Danny, but I think you're the opposite of Richard. We need something between the two. That means a woman! Yes, I think a woman might be able to do it. A stylish woman, but one who knows the difficult side of life from experience. Olga Stormer, for instance! Don't talk to me, I've got a plan coming.'

She put her face in her hands, then lifted it suddenly.

'What's the name of that girl who wants to be my <u>understudy</u>? Margaret Ryan, isn't it? The girl with the hair like mine?'

Danahan looked at Olga's beautiful, long gold hair. 'Yes, it's just like yours, as you say. But she's no good at acting. I was going to get rid of her next week.'

'Well, don't. I need her.'

Danahan didn't look happy. Olga continued anyway.

'Danny, answer me one question honestly. Do you think I can act? *Really act*, I mean. Or am I just an attractive woman who goes around in pretty dresses?'

'Act? Of course! Olga, there's been nobody like you since Duse!'

'Then if Levitt really is a coward, my plan will work. No, I'm not going to tell you about it. I want you to find the Ryan girl. Tell her I'm interested in her and want her to have dinner here tomorrow night.'

'She'll be delighted!'

Olga continued: 'The other thing I want are some strong sleeping pills that will make someone fall asleep for an hour or two.'

Danahan smiled.

'I can get those.'

'Good! Now go, Danny, and leave the rest to me.'

◆ ◆ ◆

Alone in his dark, shabby room, Jake Levitt smiled as he quickly tore open the envelope he'd been expecting.

*Dear Mr Levitt,*

*I do not remember the lady you mention, but I meet so many people that my memory is not always perfect. I am always pleased to help any actress, and I will be at home if you would like to visit me this evening at nine o'clock.*

*Yours,*

*Olga Stormer*

Levitt nodded. It was a clever note! She hadn't admitted anything; however, she was willing to talk. He felt sure that lots of money was coming his way.

At nine o'clock Levitt was standing outside the door of the actress's flat. He rang the bell.

No one answered.

He was about to ring it again when he realized that the door was not locked. He pushed it open and went into the hall. To his right was an open door leading into a bright room decorated in red and black. Levitt walked in. On the table under a lamp there was a note:

*Please wait until I return.*
O. *Stormer*

Levitt sat down and waited. He was beginning to feel nervous, which was not normal for him. The flat was very quiet. Yet there was something horrible about the silence – he had the strange feeling that he wasn't alone.

How silly!

His forehead felt wet. And the feeling grew stronger. He was sure he wasn't alone!

Annoyed, he jumped up and began to walk up and down. In a minute the woman would return and then—

He stopped suddenly with a cry. He could see a hand under the black curtains that hung across the window! He touched it. It was cold – horribly cold. It was a dead hand.

Slowly, he opened the curtains. There was a woman lying there. She had one arm out to the side and the other was underneath her. She was lying on her stomach, her long, golden hair covering her face and neck.

*Olga Stormer!*

So she had escaped him, he thought – by taking the simplest way out.

Suddenly he saw two ends of red <u>cord</u>. They were half-hidden by her hair. He touched the cords gently, trying to understand what he was looking at.

As he did, the head moved, and for a moment he saw a horrible purple face. He jumped back with a cry. There were two things here he did not understand. First, this was murder – the woman had been <u>strangled</u>; and second – *she was not Olga Stormer!*

There was a sound behind him. He turned around quickly and looked straight into the frightened eyes of a <u>maid</u>. Her face was as white as the clothes she was wearing. But he didn't fully understand the look in her eyes until she spoke:

'Oh, my! You— You've killed her!'

Even then he didn't quite realize the danger he was in. He replied:

'No, no, she was dead when I found her.'

'But I *saw* you! You pulled the cord and strangled her. I heard her cry.'

His forehead was wetter than ever now. He thought back over everything he had done in the room. The maid must have come in when he had the two ends of cord in his hands; she had seen the head move and had thought that his own cry had come from the dead girl. He looked at her again. There was no doubt about what he saw in her face – she was scared and she was stupid. She would tell the police she had seen the crime happen. She would never change her story and his life would be over because she would believe it was the truth.

What a horrible, unexpected group of events!

But wait – was it unexpected? Or had someone planned it?

Without thinking, he said:

'That's not your boss, you know.'

Her answer made everything clearer to him.

'No, it's her actress friend – if you can call them friends. All they did was fight. They were fighting tonight.'

So the whole thing was a <u>trap</u>! He understood now.

'Where's Miss Stormer?'

'She went out ten minutes ago.'

A trap! And he had walked into it like a lamb. She was a clever girl, this Olga Stormer; she had got rid of someone she didn't like, and he would be <u>charged</u> for it. Murder!

He heard a small noise. The little maid was trying to get to the door. Her brain was beginning to work again. Her eyes glanced at the telephone, then back to the door. He had no choice, he had to kill her. It was the only way. He would rather be killed for a crime he did do instead of for one he didn't.[2]

Then his heart jumped. On the table beside her, almost under her hand, lay a small gun. If he could reach it first—

But she saw him looking. As he moved forwards, she grabbed the gun and pointed it at him. He stopped moving. What could he do?

There was one thing he could do. He ran from the room, through the hall and out of the front door. He heard her voice, quiet and scared, calling, 'Police! Murder!' Down the stairs he ran, then along the quiet street, then he slowed to a walk as he saw somebody coming round the corner.

He quickly made a plan. He would go to Gravesend as quickly as possible. A boat was sailing from there that night going far away. If he gave the men working on the boat some money, they wouldn't ask any questions. He would be safe as soon as he was out at sea.

♦ ◆ ♦

Later that evening, Danahan's telephone rang. It was Olga.

'Danny, Miss Ryan is going to play my part tomorrow night. Please don't argue. I owe her something after all the things I did to her tonight!

'What? Yes, I think my problems are over now. Poor thing – I gave her lots of sleeping pills in her coffee! After that, I painted her face purple and tied her left arm so that the blood left it! She thinks I put her into a special <u>trance</u>!

'You're confused? Well, you'll have to stay confused until tomorrow. I haven't got time to explain now. I must change my clothes before my maid comes back from the cinema. There was a "beautiful drama" on tonight, she told me. But she missed the most beautiful drama of all. I played my best part tonight, Danny. Jake Levitt is definitely a coward, and oh, Danny – *I'm an actress!*'

# ◆ Character list ◆

## The Witness for the Prosecution

**Mr Mayherne:** lawyer to Leonard Vole

**Leonard Vole:** man charged with the murder of Miss Emily French

**Miss Emily French:** rich old lady who has been murdered

**Janet Mackenzie:** Miss French's maid

**Romaine Heilger:** Leonard Vole's wife

**Sir Charles:** court lawyer working on Leonard Vole's case

**Mrs Mogson:** lady who has information for Mr Mayherne about the case

## The Rajah's Emerald

**James Fleming:** young man on holiday in Kimpton-on-Sea

**Grace:** girlfriend of James. Also on holiday in Kimpton-on-Sea

**Claud Sopworth:** upper class friend of Grace's

**Clara, Alice and Dorothy Sopworth:** sisters of Claud Sopworth

**Lord Edward Campion:** owns a house in Kimpton-on-Sea

**The Rajah of Maraputna:** a foreign king and friend of Lord Campion's

**Detective-Inspector Merrilees:** a police officer

# Philomel Cottage

**Alix Martin:** wife of Gerald Martin

**Gerald Martin:** husband of Alix Martin

**Dick Windyford:** former boyfriend of Alix Martin

**George:** gardener to the Martins


# The Actress

**Jake Levitt:** man who goes to see a play at the theatre

**Olga Stormer:** famous actress

**Miss Jones:** Olga Stormer's assistant

**Syd Danahan (Danny):** Olga Stormer's manager

**Sir Richard Everard:** the man Olga Stormer is going to marry

**Margaret Ryan:** actress who works with Olga

# ◆ CULTURAL NOTES ◆

## 1. The British law system

If someone is charged with a crime, they have to go to court. This is called a trial. A lawyer is the person who will work with the charged person before the trial. In *The Witness for the Prosecution*, Mr Mayherne is *Leonard Vole*'s lawyer. The lawyer will try to find evidence and witnesses and use these to 'make a case' – to prove that the person is not guilty of the crime. This is called the defence.

On the other side, there will be lawyers who are trying to find evidence and witnesses that can prove that the person is guilty of the crime. These lawyers are called the prosecution.

In court, a different type of lawyer may speak to the jury and question witnesses – not the lawyer who prepared the case. In *The Witness for the Prosecution* the court lawyer is Sir Charles.

The jury is a group of 12 people who will listen to the lawyers for both sides, then decide if the person is guilty or innocent. They are normal people, not lawyers. The jury must all agree.

The judge is the person who decides what will happen to someone if the jury decides they are guilty.

## 2. The death penalty

When these stories were written, in the 1920s and 1930s, anyone who killed a person on purpose could be hanged by the neck. Hanging meant they tied a rope around the person's neck and then dropped them through an automatic door. Hanging by the rope, they could not breathe and died. This was called the death penalty. The death penalty for murder ended in the UK in 1965.

## 3. The British class system

When these stories were written, around the 1920s and 1930s, Britain had a class system with rules that everybody knew. Many of the *upper classes* had titles: they were Dukes, Lords, Marquesses, Earls, Viscounts and Barons. They did not usually work for a living unless they were in politics, diplomacy (working for the UK with foreign governments) or the army. In *The Rajah's Emerald, Lord Campion* is a member of this class. In *The Actress, Sir Richard Everard* is also from the upper class.

The *middle classes* were educated people who had to work for a living – in the law, medicine, education, business, the Church or something similar. *James* is middle class in *The Rajah's Emerald*. Older women rarely worked, but younger women, such as *Grace* in *The Rajah's Emerald* and *Alix* in *Philomel Cottage*, had started to take jobs in offices.

The *working classes* usually only went to school until they were fourteen. After that they were generally involved in all other work not done by the middle and upper classes. Many were employed in the houses of rich families, like *Jones*, Lord Campion's driver in *The Rajah's Emerald*.

This class system lasted until the Second World War (1939–1945) when many social rules changed, especially the role of women in society.

## 4. Philomel

Philomel is an old word for a nightingale. A nightingale is a small brown bird. It is linked with love because of its beautiful singing. It sings at night.

## 5. Cockney
A Cockney is a person who was born in the east part of London. In *Philomel Cottage*, *Gerald* refers to *Alix* as a Cockney, suggesting that she comes from East London and that because of this she doesn't know much about living in the country.

## 6. Electric lights
At the beginning of the 20<sup>th</sup> century in the UK, only rich people had electric light – most people had gas lights instead. When *Philomel Cottage* was written in 1934, ordinary people outside of the big cities were just beginning to have electric lights in their homes and it was seen as being very modern.

## 7. MP
MP stands for Member of Parliament. Parliament is where a group of people make the laws (the rules) for a country. Many upper class men (see note 3) like *Sir Richard Everard* became Members of Parliament. It is a very important job and members of parliament are meant to live perfect lives. Getting married to someone who had killed a person, as *Sir Richard Everard* is about to do in *The Actress*, would not have been allowed. He would have had to leave his job in parliament.

# ◆ GLOSSARY ◆

**acid** VARIABLE NOUN
An **acid** is a liquid that can damage your skin and clothes.

**alibi** COUNTABLE NOUN
If you have an **alibi**, you can prove that you were somewhere else when a crime took place.

**ass** COUNTABLE NOUN
In informal English, if you call someone an **ass**, you mean that they are behaving in a silly way.

**badge** COUNTABLE NOUN
A **badge** is a small piece of metal or cloth showing a picture or words, which you attach to your clothes.

**bang people's heads together** PHRASE
If you **bang people's heads together**, you tell them off for doing something wrong or for not doing something they were asked to do.

**beach hut** COUNTABLE NOUN
A **beach hut** is a small building on a beach used for getting changed and storing things.

**beg** TRANSITIVE VERB
If you **beg** someone to do something, you are very keen for someone to do it.

**bigamist** COUNTABLE NOUN
A **bigamist** is a person who marries someone when they are already married to someone else.

**boarding house** COUNTABLE NOUN
A **boarding house** is a house which people pay to stay in for a short time.

**burglar** COUNTABLE NOUN
A **burglar** is a thief who breaks into houses and steals things.

**business-like** ADJECTIVE
If you describe someone as **business-like**, you mean that they deal with things in an efficient way, as if they were running a business.

**carrion crow** COUNTABLE NOUN
A **carrion crow** is a type of large black bird which eats the meat of dead animals.

**case** COUNTABLE NOUN
When talking about a crime, the **case** for or against someone is all of the things that are known about what happened.

**cellar** COUNTABLE NOUN
A **cellar** is a room underneath a building.

**charge** TRANSITIVE VERB
When the police **charge** someone, they say that that person has done something illegal.

**client** COUNTABLE NOUN
A **client** is someone for whom a professional person or organization is doing some work.

**cord** VARIABLE NOUN
A **cord** is a strong, thick string.

**court** COUNTABLE NOUN
A **court** is a place where questions to do with the law are decided by a judge.

**coward** COUNTABLE NOUN
A **coward** is someone who is easily frightened and avoids dangerous or difficult situations.

**crowbar** COUNTABLE NOUN
A **crowbar** is a heavy iron bar.

**develop** TRANSITIVE VERB
When a camera film is **developed**, photographs are made from it.

**duke** COUNTABLE NOUN
A **duke** is a person who belongs to a high social group.

**dynamic** ADJECTIVE
A **dynamic** person is full of energy.

**emerald** COUNTABLE NOUN
An **emerald** is a bright green valuable stone.

**emotional** ADJECTIVE
When someone is **emotional**, they show their feelings, especially because they are upset.

**evidence** UNCOUNTABLE NOUN
**Evidence** is information which is used to prove that something is true.

**fascinated** ADJECTIVE
If you are **fascinated** by something, you find it very interesting, and you think about it a lot.

**fête** COUNTABLE NOUN
A **fête** is an event held outside that includes competitions and people selling goods that have been made at home.

**get off** PHRASAL VERB
If someone who has broken a law or rule **gets off**, they are not punished, or only punished a bit.

**guilty** ADJECTIVE
If someone is **guilty** of a crime, they have done the crime.

**hanged** TRANSITIVE VERB
If someone is **hanged**, they are killed by having a rope tied around their neck.

**impulsive** ADJECTIVE
Someone who is **impulsive** does things suddenly without thinking about them carefully first.

**innocent** ADJECTIVE
If someone is **innocent**, they did not do a crime which other people said they did.

**investments** COUNTABLE NOUN
An **investment** is an amount of money that you put into something like a bank to increase its value.

**jewel** COUNTABLE NOUN
A **jewel** is a valuable stone used in things such as rings or necklaces.

**jury** COUNTABLE NOUN
In a court, the **jury** is the group of people who have been chosen from the general public to listen to the facts about a crime and to decide whether a person is guilty or not.

**maid** COUNTABLE NOUN
A **maid** is a woman who works for a person or family in their home.

**make up** PHRASAL VERB
If you **make up** a story, you try to make other people think it is true when it is not.

**miserably** ADVERB
If you do or say something **miserably**, you do or say it unhappily.

**mole** COUNTABLE NOUN
A **mole** is a dark spot on someone's skin that they are born with.

**mortgage** COUNTABLE NOUN
A **mortgage** is a loan of money which you get from a bank in order to buy a house.

**mute** COUNTABLE NOUN
The **mute** key on a telephone is the button that stops the other person from hearing what you are saying.

**nightingale** COUNTABLE NOUN
A **nightingale** is a small brown bird.

**nod** INTRANSITIVE VERB
If you **nod**, you move your head down and up to show that you understand or like something, or that you agree with it.

**panic** INTRANSITIVE VERB
If you **panic**, you become nervous or afraid, and act without thinking carefully.

**poison** VARIABLE NOUN
**Poison** is something that harms or kills people or animals if they swallow it.

**pretend** TRANSITIVE VERB
If you **pretend** that something is true, you try to make people believe that it is true, although it is not.

**prosecution** SINGULAR NOUN
The lawyers who try to prove that a person is guilty are called the **prosecution**.

**proud** ADJECTIVE
Someone who is **proud** knows their own importance and value.

**psychiatric** ADJECTIVE
**Psychiatric** means involving mental illness.

**Rajah** COUNTABLE NOUN
In India, a **Rajah** was a prince or other important person.

**revenge** UNCOUNTABLE NOUN
**Revenge** involves hurting someone who has hurt you.

**scar** COUNTABLE NOUN
A **scar** is a mark on the skin which is left after a wound has got better.

**shabby** ADJECTIVE
If something or someone is **shabby**, they look old, dirty or untidy.

**shake one's head** TRANSITIVE VERB
If you **shake your head**, you move it from side to side in order to show that you are unhappy with something.

**spade** COUNTABLE NOUN
A **spade** is a tool used for digging, with a flat metal blade and a long handle.

**strangely** ADVERB
If someone does something **strangely**, what they do is a bit unusual.

**strangle** TRANSITIVE VERB
To **strangle** someone means to kill them by tightly squeezing their throat.

**subconscious** ADJECTIVE
Your **subconscious** mind is the part of your mind that can make you do or think something without realizing it.

**suspicious** ADJECTIVE
If you describe someone or something as **suspicious**, you mean that there is something about them which makes you think that they have done something they shouldn't have.

**sway** INTRANSITIVE VERB
When people or things **sway**, they move slowly from one side to the other.

**swindle** TRANSITIVE VERB
If someone **swindles** a person or an organization, they try to get money from them.

**swindler** COUNTABLE NOUN
A **swindler** is someone who is swindling another person or organization.

**thank goodness** PHRASE
You say **thank goodness** when you are very happy that something bad has not happened.

**the shoe is on the other foot**
PHRASE
If you say that **the shoe is on the other foot**, you mean that a situation has been changed completely, so that the person who was in the better position before is now in the worse one.

**trance** COUNTABLE NOUN
If someone is in a **trance**, they seem to be asleep, but they can see and hear things.

**trap** COUNTABLE NOUN
A **trap** is a trick so that you do or say something which you did not want to.

**trial** COUNTABLE NOUN
A **trial** is when a judge listens to evidence and decides whether a person is guilty of a crime.

**tropical** ADJECTIVE
**Tropical** means belonging to or coming from a part of the world called 'the Tropics'. Tropical plants and flowers are often very colourful and bright.

**understudy** COUNTABLE NOUN
An **understudy** is the person who has learned a part in a play and can act the part if the actor or actress is ill.

**will** COUNTABLE NOUN
A **will** is a legal document saying what you want to happen to your money and the things that you own when you die.

**witness** COUNTABLE NOUN
A **witness** is someone who appears in court to say what they know about a crime or other event.

**you could have heard a pin drop** PHRASE
You can say **you could have heard a pin drop** when a place is very quiet, especially when someone has said or done something shocking.

**COLLINS ENGLISH READERS ONLINE**

Go online to discover the following useful resources for teachers and students:

- Downloadable audio of the story

- Classroom activities, including a plot synopsis

- Student activities, suitable for class use or for self-studying learners

- A level checker to ensure you are reading at the correct level

- Information on the Collins COBUILD Grading Scheme

All this and more at **www.collinselt.com/readers**

**COLLINS ENGLISH READERS**

**Do you want to read more at your reading level?
Try these:**

## AGATHA CHRISTIE MYSTERIES

Death on the Nile  978-0-00-824968-7
Murder on the Orient Express  978-0-00-824967-0
The Body in the Library  978-0-00-824969-4
Dead Man's Folly  978-0-00-824970-0

## OTHER LEVEL 3 COLLINS ENGLISH READERS

Amazing Scientists  978-0-00-754510-0
Amazing Philanthropists  978-0-00-754504-9
Amazing Performers  978-0-00-754505-6
Amazing Explorers  978-0-00-754497-4
Amazing Writers  978-0-00-754498-1

**Are you ready for Level 4? Use our online level checker to find out.**

Find out more at **www.collinselt.com/readers**